Hurray for Barbara Park
and the Junie B. Jones® books!

"Park, one of the funniest writers around . . . brings her refreshing humor to the beginning chapter-book set." —*Booklist*

"Park is simply hilarious."
—America Online's *The Book Report*

"Park has a wonderful ear for the dialogue of five-year-olds and an even better grasp of how their minds operate." —*Booklist*

"Park is truly a funny writer. Although Junie B. is a kindergartner, she's sure to make middle graders laugh out loud." —*School Library Journal*

"Junie's swarms of young fans will continue to delight in her unique take on the world. . . . A hilarious, first-rate read-aloud." —*Kirkus Reviews*

"Junie B. is a darling of the young-reader set."
—*USA Today*

"The honesty and inventiveness of this savvy kindergartner make the Junie B. books accessible and completely enjoyable." —*School Library Journal*

Laugh out loud with Junie B. Jones!

**Check out Barbara Park's other great books,
listed at the end of this book!**

Junie B. Jones®
and some
Sneaky Peeky Spying

BY BARBARA PARK

illustrated by
Denise Brunkus

A STEPPING STONE BOOK™

Random House 🏠 New York

To my editor, Linda Hayward—
Junie B.'s bestest real-life friend

Library of Congress Cataloging-in-Publication Data
Park, Barbara.
Junie B. Jones and some sneaky peeky spying / by Barbara Park ; illustrated by Denise Brunkus.
  p. cm. "A stepping stone book."
SUMMARY: Six-year-old Junie B.'s penchant for spying on people and her curiosity about the private life of her teacher get her in trouble in kindergarten.
ISBN 978-0-679-85101-1 (pbk.) — ISBN 978-0-679-95101-8 (lib. bdg.)
[1. Kindergarten—Fiction. 2. Schools—Fiction. 3. Teachers—Fiction.
4. Humorous stories.] I. Brunkus, Denise, ill. II. Title.
PZ7.P2197Jts 1994 [Fic]—dc20 93-5557

Printed in the United States of America
47 46 45 44 43 42 41 40

Contents

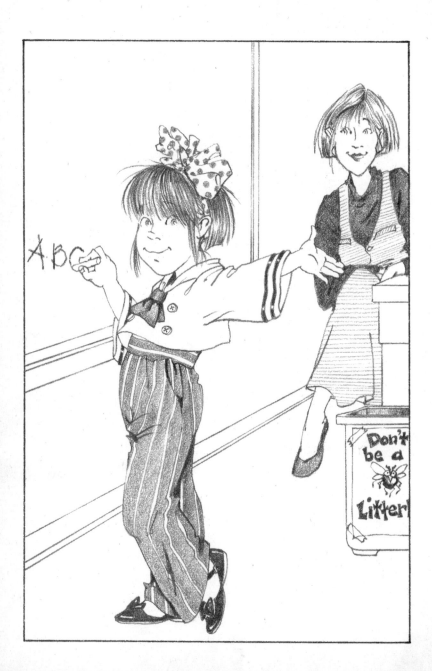

1/Sneaky Peeky Spying

My name is Junie B. Jones. The B stands for Beatrice. Except I don't like Beatrice. I just like B and that's all.

I go to kindergarten. Kindergarten is what comes before first grade. Except for I don't know why it's called that silly word of kindergarten. 'Cause it should be called zero grade, I think.

My teacher has the name of Mrs.

She has another name, too. But I just like Mrs. and that's all.

Mrs. has short brown hair. And long skirts of wool. And she smiles a real lot.

Except for sometimes when I'm noisy, she claps her loud hands at me.

It used to scare me very much. Only then I got used to it. And now I don't even pay it any attention.

I wish Mrs. lived next door to me.

Then me and her would be neighbors.

And bestest friends.

And also I could spy on her.

Spying is when you be very quiet. And you look at people through a peeky hole or a crack or something.

I am a very good spier.

That's because I have sneaky feet. And my nose doesn't whistle when I breathe.

Last Friday morning at Grampa Miller's house, I hided in the dirty clothes hamper.

Then my grampa came in the bathroom. And I lifted up the lid a teeny bit. And I peeked my eyes at him.

And guess what?

Grampa Miller took his whole teeth right out of his head! That's what!

I popped right out of the hamper!

"HEY! GRAMPA! HOW DID YOU DO THAT CRAZY THING!" I hollered.

Then my grampa screamed very loud. And he runned out of the bathroom speedy quick.

Grampa Miller has high blood pressure, I think.

Pretty soon Mother hurried into the bath-room with angry feet.

"That's it!" she yelled. "No more spying! This is the last time I'm telling you! Do you hear me, missy? Do you?"

"Yes," I said. "'Cause you're hollering right in my ear, that's why."

Then Mother took me home. Except for she kept on staying mad at me.

"Find something quiet to do," she said kind of growly. "Your baby brother has to take his morning nap."

So then I thought and thought about what

to do. And a very great idea popped into my head.

First, I took off my loud shoes…

Then I tippy-toed into baby Ollie's room in just my sock feet…

And I spied on him through the bars in his crib.

'Cause what could be quieter than sneaky peeky spying, of course!

Only too bad for me. Because that boring old baby just kept on sleeping and sleeping.

And he wasn't being fun.

So that's how come I accidentally blowed on his face.

And I tickled his nose with a ribbon.

And I shouted, "WAKE UP!" in his ear.

And guess what? Ollie opened his eyes, that's what!

Then he started crying very loud. And Mother runned into his room.

Only she didn't even see me!

'Cause I quick hided in the closet!

I smiled to just myself. I'm the bestest spier in the whole wide world, I said inside my head.

That's how come—when I rode the bus to school that day—I did a little bit of bragging.

"I'm the bestest spier in the whole world," I said to my bestest friend named Grace.

Then I took off my shoes. And I showed her my sneaky sock feet.

"See?" I said. "See how quiet they are? You can hardly even hear those guys."

After that, I breathed in and out for her.

"And see? My nose doesn't whistle, either," I said.

That Grace smiled. "I'm good at spying, too," she said.

I patted her. "Yeah, only too bad, Grace.

But you can't be as good as me. 'Cause I said it first."

That Grace did a mad breath at me. It is called a huffy, I think.

"I heard your nose whistle, Grace," I told her.

Just then the bus got to school. And me and that Grace raced each other to the playground.

Except for she beated me. Only it didn't count. 'Cause I wasn't really racing.

Then we played horses with my other bestest friend named Lucille. Only pretty soon the bell rang. And we all runned to Room Nine speedy quick.

Mrs. was at the door waiting for us.

"Good afternoon, ladies," she said.

"Good afternoon, lady," I said back very polite.

Then Mrs. smiled at me.

That's because she is the nicest teacher I ever saw.

And so I wish me and her were bestest friends.

And guess what else?

I wish I could hide in her hamper.

2/Questions

Me and my bestest friend Lucille sit at my same table together.

My table is where I sit up straight.

And do my work.

And don't talk to my neighbor.

Except I keep on forgetting that part.

"I wonder where Mrs. lives?" I whispered to Lucille real quiet.

"Shh," said Lucille. "We can't talk or else we'll get in trouble. And anyway, you're not allowed to know where she lives. 'Cause it's a secret."

"Says who?" I asked.

"Says my brother, that's who. And he's in third grade. And he says teachers have to keep their house a secret. Or else kids might go there and throw rotten tomatoes."

I did a huffy at her.

"Yeah, only I don't want to throw rotten tomatoes, Lucille," I explained. "I just want to hide in her hamper, and that's all."

"I don't care," she said. "You're still not allowed. 'Cause my brother said so. And he knows more than you do. So there."

I made an angry face. "*So there* is not a nice word, Lucille," I said.

Then I made a fist at her. Except for Mrs. saw me. And so I had to unfold it.

After that I behaved myself very good. I sat up real straight. And I did all my work.

Work is when you use your brain and a pencil.

Only sometimes I accidentally use the eraser too hard. And a big hole rubs in my paper.

"Hey! I did beautifully today!" I called out. "'Cause guess what? No hole! That's what!"

Mrs. came to my table. She put a gold star on my work.

"You *did* do beautifully, Junie B.," she said. "Maybe I'll hang this one on the wall for Grandparents' Day on Monday. Would you like that?"

"Yes," I said. "Only I keep on forgetting how come those guys are coming to this place."

Then Mrs. explained to me all about Grandparents' Day again.

She said our grandparents are coming for a visit. And we get to show them Room Nine. And also we get to have 'freshments together.

Mrs. said 'freshments are cookies and abeverage.

I raised my hand.

"Yeah, only I don't think I'm allowed to have the kind of drink named abeverage. 'Cause I'm only allowed to have milk and juice and that's all."

Mrs. looked up at the ceiling with her eyes. Then I looked up there, too. But I didn't see anything.

"How many of you think you can bring cookies on Monday?" asked Mrs.

"I CAN! I CAN!" I hollered very excited. "'CAUSE MY MOTHER IS THE BESTEST COOKIE BAKER IN THE WHOLE

WORLD, THAT'S WHY! EXCEPT FOR ONE TIME SHE ACCIDENTALLY FORGOT THEY WERE IN THE OVEN. AND THE FIREMEN HAD TO COME TO OUR HOUSE."

Mrs. laughed. Only I don't know why. 'Cause that was not a funny story.

After that, she gave me a note for Mother. It was some writing about baking cookies, I think.

"If your mother has any questions, please tell her to call me," said Mrs.

Just then I got a very great idea!

"Hey!" I said. "Maybe me and Mother can bring the cookies to your house! And so then I can see where you live!"

Mrs. rumpled my hair. "You don't have to come to my house, Junie B. Just bring the cookies to school on Monday morning."

I smiled very sweet. "Yeah, only I still want to see where you live," I said.

Then Mrs. turned around. And she walked back to her desk.

That's how come I had to follow her.

"Do you have the rich kind of house? Or the regular kind of house?" I asked her. "'Cause I just have the regular kind of house.

Except for Mother wants the rich kind. Only Daddy said *lotsa luck*."

Mrs. pointed at my chair. That means to sit down, I think.

"Yeah, only do you have a daddy that lives at your house, too? Are there any pictures of him in your wallet? Let's look in there, okay? Do you have a secret compartment in it? 'Cause my grampa Miller has one of those things with fifty bucks in it. Only don't tell Grandma."

Mrs. took my hand. Then me and her walked back to my table.

"Yeah, only guess what I'm wondering now? Now I'm wondering what your bedtime is. 'Cause my bedtime is when the little hand is at the seven, and the big hand is at the six. Only I hate that dumb stupid bedtime. 'Cause I'm not even tired yet, of course."

Mrs. put her finger up to her lips.

"That's enough, Junie B.," she said. "I mean it. I want you to settle down now."

Then she went right back to the front of the room. And she didn't answer any of my questions.

'Cause guess why?

Mrs. is a secret mystery guy. That's why.

3/ Secret Mystery Guy

Me and my bestest friend Grace rode the bus home together.

That's when I told her about Mrs. and her secret house.

"Mrs. is a secret mystery guy," I said. "'Cause she wouldn't answer any of my questions. And so now I have curiosity about her."

That Grace wrinkled her eyebrows. "Me, too," she said. "Now I have curiosity about her, too."

I patted her again. "Yeah, only too bad,

Grace. But you can't have as much as me. 'Cause I said it first, remember that?"

That Grace did another huffy at me.

"Whoops. Your nose is still whistling, Grace," I said.

A few minutes later, I got off the bus. I runned to my house like a speedy rocket.

"GRANDMA! GRANDMA!" I shouted very excited. "IT'S ME! IT'S JUNIE B. JONES! I'M HOME FROM MY SCHOOL!"

Grandma Miller babysits me and baby Ollie when Mother is at work.

She was in the kitchen feeding Ollie sprained peas.

"GUESS WHAT, GRANDMA! GUESS WHAT? MY TEACHER IS A SECRET MYSTERY GUY! AND SHE WON'T TELL ME WHERE SHE LIVES. ONLY I WANT TO GO TO HER HOUSE VERY BAD!"

20

Grandma Miller shushed me. "There's no need to shout, Junie B.," she said. "I'm right here."

"Yeah, only I can't help it, Grandma! 'Cause I have curiosity about her!"

Grandma Miller did a little smile. "Curiosity killed the cat, you know," she said.

Then my mouth went open. And my eyes got very big too.

"What cat, Grandma? Where did the curiosity kill it? Was it in the street by my school? 'Cause I saw a squished cat in the street by my school. Only Paulie Allen Puffer said it got runned over by the ice cream truck."

Grandma Miller looked at me for a very long time. Then she went to the sink. And she took an aspirin.

Just then I heard a noise at the front door.

And its name is Mother was home from work!

"MOTHER! MOTHER! I HAVE A 'PORTANT NOTE FROM MRS. 'CAUSE YOU AND ME ARE GOING TO BAKE DELICIOUS COOKIES. AND THEN WE CAN TAKE THEM TO HER HOUSE AND SEE WHERE SHE LIVES!"

Mother read the note.

"The note says to take the cookies to school, Junie B. Not to your teacher's house."

"Yeah, only I already know that. But my teacher is a secret mystery guy. And she won't tell me where she lives. And so you and me have to find it ourselves."

Mother shook her head. "No way, toots," she said.

"Yes way!" I hollered. "We have to!

'Cause now I've got curiosity in me. And I have to find out where her house is. Or else Grandma said I'm gonna get runned over by an ice cream truck."

Then Mother did a frown at Grandma. And Grandma took another aspirin.

"Your teacher is *not* a secret mystery guy, Junie B.," said Mother. "She's just a regular person. With a regular family. And there's no way that you and I are going to bother her at her house."

I stamped my foot. "YES WE ARE! WE ARE TOO! 'CAUSE I WANT TO, THAT'S WHY!"

After that, I got sended to my room.

'Cause of no shouting. And no stamping my foot. Only I never even heard of that dumb rule before.

I shut my door very angry. Then I put my

head under my pillow. And I called Mother the name of pewie head.

"And guess what else?" I said very quiet. "Teachers are not regular people.

"So there. Ha ha."

4/ Cookie Mix and Other Stuff

The next day was Saturday.

Saturday is the day me and my mother go to the grocery store.

I have rules at that place.

Like no hollering the words I WANT ICE CREAM!

And no calling Mother the name of big meanie when she won't buy it.

And no eating a bag of marshmallows that doesn't belong to you.

Or else the store guy yanks it away from you. And he says, *Eating is the same thing as stealing, young lady.*

Then he takes you to Mother. And she has to pay for the whole entire bag. Except for I don't know why. 'Cause I only ate three of those softy guys and that's all.

The carts at the grocery store have seats in them. That's where babies sit. Only not me. 'Cause big girls get to walk all by theirselves.

And guess what else? One time Mother even let me push the whole big cart without any help.

Except for then some baked beanies got knocked off their shelf. And a grandma got her foot caught in my tire. And so now I have to wait till I'm bigger.

My favorite aisle is where the cookies are.

That's 'cause sometimes there is a lady at a table there. And she gives me and Mother cookie samples. And we don't even have to pay for them.

Their name is freebies, I think.

Only too bad for me. 'Cause this time the lady wasn't there.

"Darn it," I said very disappointed. "No freebie lady."

Mother smiled. "That's okay. When we get home, we're going to bake our own cookies for Grandparents' Day, remember? Won't that be fun?" she asked.

I made my shoulders go up and down.

That's 'cause I was still mad at her for not taking me to my teacher's house, of course.

"What kind of cookie mix do you want?" asked Mother.

I did a frown at her. "I don't even want to

bake cookies anymore," I said. "'Cause you still won't take me to where Mrs. lives."

Mother rumpled my hair. "Staying mad isn't going to change things, Junie B.," she said. "Now do you want to pick out the cookie mix? Or shall I?"

Then Mother picked out some cookie mix. And she gave it to me. And I throwed it in the cart very hard.

"Thank you," said Mother.

"You're not welcome," I said.

After that, Mother took me outside of the store. And me and her had a little talk.

A little talk is when Mother is mad at me. And she says who do I think I am, missy? And zactly how long do I think she's going to put up with me?

Then I have to say a 'pology to her.

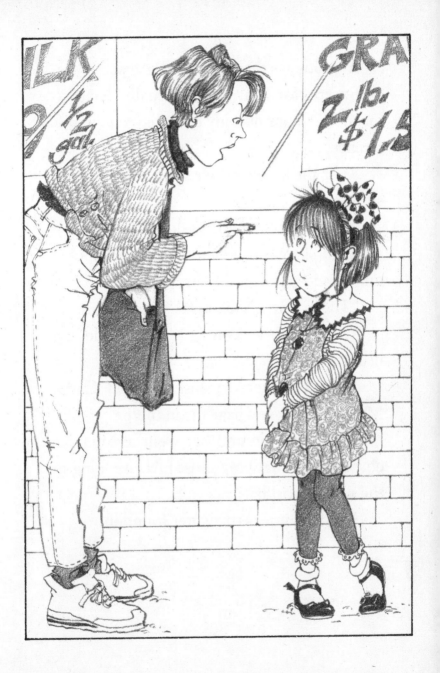

A 'pology is the words *I'm sorry.*

Except for you don't actually have to mean it. 'Cause nobody can even tell the difference.

After the little talk, we went back into the store.

"Shall we try again?" asked Mother.

Then she gave me another box of cookie mix. And I put it in the cart very nice.

"That's better," she said. "Thank you."

You're not welcome, I said inside my head.

Then I smiled to just myself. 'Cause Mother can't even hear me in there.

After that, me and her went around the corner. And I saw my most favorite thing in the whole world!

And its name is the water fountain!

"Hey! I need a drink!" I said very excited.

Then I runned right over there. And I hopped up on the little step.

"Need some help?" called Mother.

"No," I said. "'Cause I'm almost six years old, that's why. And so I already know how to work this big guy.

"And here's another thing I know," I said. "No putting your mouth on the water spout. Or else germs will get inside you. And you will die."

I smiled very proud. "Paulie Allen Puffer told me that," I explained.

Then I bended my head over the fountain. And I drank for a very long time.

"Hurry up, Junie B.," said Mother. "I need to get the shopping done."

I wiped my mouth off with my arm.

"Yeah, only I can't hurry up. Or else I might get a stomachache and spit up water. 'Cause a boy named William did that on the playground yesterday."

Mother looked at her watch. "Okay. Well, I'm going to be right here in the cereal aisle. As soon as you've finished drinking, come directly back to me."

"Okey-dokey," I said very happy.

Then I turned around and drinked and drinked and drinked.

Except for then I started feeling a little bit sickish. And so I had to sit down on the little step and rest my water.

That's when the big front doors of the grocery store opened.

And guess what?

My eyes almost popped out of my head, that's what!

'Cause I saw a big shock!

And its name was Mrs.!

My real live teacher named Mrs. was at the grocery store!!!

5/Sickish

Mrs. didn't see me.

That's because I hided behind the water fountain speedy fast.

And guess what?

She had a *man* with her!

And I never even saw that guy before!

"Hey! Who the heck is that?" I said to just myself.

Then I runned my fastest to the cereal aisle, to tell Mother what I saw.

Only all of a sudden I remembered about

how she told me *no more spying*. And so maybe I might get in trouble with her, I think.

That's how come I stopped running. And I started to go back to peek at Mrs. some more. But Mother already spotted me.

"Hey! Where are you going?" she called at me. "Come here."

"Yeah, only I can't come there," I explained. "'Cause I just remembered something very important. And it's called—I'm not done drinking yet!"

Then I runned right back to the water fountain. Only Mrs. and the strange man were already disappeared.

"Shoot," I said. "Where did those Sneaky Petes go to?"

After that I had to look all over the store for those guys.

First, I looked where the chocolate milk was. Then I looked where the pasketti and tomato sauce was. And I also looked where the delicious candy was.

Only guess where I finally found them?

At the stinky dumb vegetables! That's where!

I quick ducked down and hided around the corner.

Then I did some sneaky peeky spying on them.

I saw Mrs. picking out yucky blucky brockly.

And stewie pewie tomatoes.

And also the kind of vegetable named Sue Keeny.

Except for then the strange man snatched Sue Keeny right out of her hands. And he tried to put it back on the shelf.

Only Mrs. grabbed it right back again.

And she pretended to hit him on the head with it. And then they both started laughing very much.

That's when a very terrible thing happened.

And it's called—Mrs. and the strange man did a big smoochie kiss!

And it was in front of the whole entire everybody!

I covered my eyes. That's 'cause I was shamed of her, of course. On account of teachers shouldn't do that smoochie thing!

After that, I peeked my eyes between my fingers. And I saw Mrs. standing at the grapes.

She picked up a bunch of the green kind. Then she pulled some grapes right off the top of it.

And that's when the most terriblest thing of all happened!

Because just then, Mrs. put the grapes in her mouth!

And she ATE them!

Mrs. ATE the GRAPES!

And she didn't even PAY for them!

"Oh no," I whispered very upset. "Oh no. Oh no."

'Cause eating is the same thing as stealing, remember?

And teachers aren't supposed to do stealing! Teachers are supposed to be perfecter than that! 'Cause they have to set a good zample for little children!

After that I felt very sickish inside of my stomach.

On account of Mrs. didn't even get caught and learn her lesson!

'Cause nobody saw what she did!

Not the store guy.

Not the strange man.

Nobody.

Nobody except for me.

6/ Squeezy Lips

I didn't tattletale on Mrs.

That's 'cause if I told Mother, I would get in trouble for spying.

And if I told the store guy, Mrs. might go to jail.

And so I just kept it a secret inside my head.

'Cause nobody can see secrets inside your head.

Not even if they look in your ears.

On Sunday Grandma and Grampa Miller

came to our house for dinner. Only I couldn't talk to them that much.

That's because secrets are very slippery. And I didn't want it to slip out of my mouth by accident.

"Why so quiet tonight, Junie B.?" said Grandma Miller at the table. "Cat got your tongue?"

My mouth went wide open.

"What cat, Grandma? Is it the same cat that got killed by the ice cream truck? How come he wants to get my tongue? Did his tongue get squished in the accident?"

Grandma Miller made a face. Then she didn't eat her roast beef anymore.

Mother looked surprised at me. "You sure did get chatty all of a sudden. Does this mean you're not mad about the cookies any-more?"

And so then I remembered to stop talking

again. Or else my secret might slip out.

I squeezed my lips together very tight.

And guess what else? Even the next day—when I was on the bus to school—my lips still stayed squeezed.

"Hi, Junie B.," said my bestest friend Grace.

I did a wave at her.

That Grace frowned at me. "How come you're not saying hi? You *have* to say hi. It's the rules."

Except for I still didn't say hi.

And so then she called me the name of big stinky.

And when we got to school, that Grace told Lucille I was being a meanie. And so those two played horses all by theirselves.

And not me.

That's how come I finally had to sing something very loud at them.

"I'VE GOT A SECRET! HA-HAHA-HA-HAAAA-HAAA," I sang.

That Grace put her hands on her hips.

"So?" she said. "We don't care. Do we, Lucille?"

Except for just then Lucille runned over to me speedy quick. 'Cause she cared, that's why.

"If you tell me your secret, I'll be your best friend," she said.

"Yeah, only I can't, Lucille," I explained. "'Cause if I tell you my secret, Mrs. might get in big trouble. And so I have to keep it inside my head."

Lucille did a frown at me.

"It's not good to keep secrets inside your head, Junie B.," she said. "My brother says keeping secrets inside your head makes pressure in there. And pretty soon your head blows up."

My eyes got very big at her.

"Oh no!" I hollered real upset.

Then I holded my head real tight with my hands. And I runned my very fastest to the nurse's office. 'Cause she has Band-Aids to hold your head together, I think.

"MY HEAD'S GONNA BLOW! MY HEAD'S GONNA BLOW!" I yelled at the nurse.

She jumped up from her desk and hurried over to me.

"What's wrong, Junie B.? Do you have a bad headache?" she asked.

"No. I have a bad *secret*. It's about Mrs. Only I can't tell anybody! And now there's pressure in my head. And I need a Band-Aid. Or else it's gonna splode!"

The nurse said calm down to me. Then she put a Band-Aid on my head. And me and her went to Principal's office.

Principal is the boss of the school.

Me and him know each other very good.

That's because I keep on getting sent down there. And so now I'm not even afraid of that guy.

Principal sat me in a big wood chair.

"Good afternoon, Junie B.," he said. "What's the trouble today?"

"Good afternoon," I said back. "My head's gonna blow."

Principal frowned his eyes at me. "Why do you think that?" he asked.

I did a little bit of squirming. "'Cause I got a secret in there, that's why," I said.

Principal sat down at his big desk. He folded his hands.

"Maybe if you tell me your secret, I can help you," he said.

"Yeah, only I can't talk," I told him.

Principal looked disappointed at me. "But I thought you and I were pals," he said.

"We are," I said. "I'm not even afraid of you."

Principal did a chuckle. "Good. That's

good," he said. "Then why don't you tell me what's bothering you."

That's when I did a huffy breath at him.

'Cause the guy wasn't listening to me, of course.

"Yeah, only I already said I can't talk, remember that? 'Cause if I talk, then I might accidentally tell you that my teacher stoled grapes at the grocery store. And then she might have to go to jail. And so that's how come I just have to keep it a secret inside my head. And that's all."

I smoothed my skirt. "The end," I said.

Then I squeezed my lips together very tight. Or else my secret might slip out.

Only guess what?

I think it already did.

7/ Sour Grapes

Principal called Mrs. to come to his office.

Only I didn't even know he was going to do that sneaky thing.

That's how come I had to pull my skirt way over my head. Or else Mrs. would see me there. And she would know I tattletaled on her.

"Don't do that," said Principal.

"Yeah, only I'm allowed," I said from underneath my skirt. "'Cause I have on my new red tights. And also boxer shorts."

After that, Principal went out of his office. And I heard my teacher's voice outside the door.

Then I quick got down from my big wood chair. And I hided under Principal's giant desk. 'Cause I was scared of what was going to happen, that's why.

I stayed quiet for lots of minutes.

Then I heard feet come back in the office.
And so I made my breath very quiet.

"Junie? Junie B. Jones?" said Principal.

"She might be hiding," said Mrs. "She's good at that, you know."

And so just then I had to think of something very quick. Or else they might come looking for me, I think.

"Yeah, only Junie B. Jones isn't hiding," I said in a scary voice. "Junie B. Jones had to go home. Only don't call her mother. Or else she will get mad at you and crack your head open."

After that, feet walked real fast around the desk. It was Principal.

"Come out of there right now, young lady," he said.

I peeked my eyes at him.

"Shoot," I said very quiet.

Then I had to sit in the big wood chair again. And Mrs. sat down next to me. Except for I didn't look at her. Or else she might be making a fist at me.

"Good afternoon, Junie B.," she said in a nice voice.

I did a gulp.

"I think you and I need to have a little talk," she said.

Then my eyes got a teeny bit of wet in them. 'Cause a little talk means I'm gonna get yelled at.

"Yeah, only I tried not to tattletale on you," I said very quick. "'Cause I didn't want you to go to jail for stealing grapes. And so I kept it a secret inside my head. And I didn't talk. And Grandma Miller thought a dead cat got my tongue.

"Only today Lucille said my head was gonna blow. And so that's how come I runned to the nurse for a Band-Aid. And she tooked me to Principal. And then my secret accidentally slipped out of my lips."

Mrs. dried my eyes with a tissue.

"It's okay, Junie B.," she said. "I'm not

angry at you. I just need to know what you saw me do at the grocery store. Can you tell me what you saw?"

Then she said the word *egg-zactly*.

I made my voice very whispering. "I egg-zactly saw you eat grapes," I told her. "Except for you didn't pay the store man for them. You just put them in your mouth and ate them. And that is called the word of stealing, I think."

After that I hided my head under my skirt again.

"You don't have to hide, Junie B.," said Mrs. "*I'm* the one who should be hiding. *I'm* the one who took the grapes."

I peeked my eyes over my skirt at her.

Then Mrs. did a little smile. And she explained all about what happened.

"Two weeks ago I bought some grapes at the grocery store," she said. "But when I got them home I discovered they were so sour no one in my family would eat them.

"So *this* week—when my husband and I went back to the store—I thought I'd be smart and taste a couple of grapes before I bought them."

I raised my eyebrows. "Is that the rules?" I asked very quiet.

Mrs. shook her head.

"No," she said. "That's *not* the rules. I should have told the grocery man about my sour grapes. And then I should have asked him if I could sample one or two. But I didn't do that. And it was right of you to worry when you saw me eating them without paying for them."

"It was?" I asked.

Mrs. smiled again. "Of course it was," she said. "It shows you know right from wrong. And it also shows that teachers make mistakes just like everybody else. Teachers aren't perfect, Junie B. *No* one is perfect."

After that I felt relief in me. 'Cause of no more secret, that's why.

"Yeah, and guess what else I saw?" I said very happy. "I saw you and your strange man do a big smoochie kiss. And it was right in front of the whole entire everybody! Only you didn't even know I was spying on you! 'Cause I'm not actually allowed to do that sneaky thing. Only my mother never even finded out!"

I smiled very proud of myself.

Except for Mrs. didn't smile back.

And Principal didn't smile back, too.
'Cause guess why?
Another secret just slipped out.
That's why.

8/Grandparents' Day

Mrs. went back to Room Nine. That's because the bell rang to start kindergarten, of course.

Only Principal didn't let me go too.

He said to stay in my wood chair.

Then he called Mother on the telephone. And he told her all about the grocery store. And also about my sneaky peeky spying.

Principal is a squealer.

After that, Mother said she wanted to talk to me. Only when I said hi, she didn't even say hi back.

She said she wasn't very happy with me, missy. And no more spying means no more spying. And we would talk about this after her work.

Then Mother said she never wants to get any more phone calls from Principal. Did I understand? Did I? Did I?

I looked at Principal.

"Mother says not to call her anymore," I told him.

Then Mother did a loud groan in the phone. Except I don't know why.

After that, me and her hanged up. And Principal said I could go to Room Nine. And so I runned there speedy quick.

Only too bad for me. 'Cause I got there

too late to sing "My Country Tizzy Thee…
Sweet Land of Liver Free." Which is my
favorite flag song.

And so I just had to sit down at my table,
and that's all.

I showed Lucille my Band-Aid.

"See? My head's not blowed up," I said
very happy.

"Too bad," said a mean boy named Jim.

I made a fist at him.

Then me and him got into a scuffle.

Scuffle is the school word for I accidentally tore his shirt.

Only guess what? I didn't even get in
trouble!

'Cause just then the grandparents came to
Room Nine for Grandparents' Day!

"HEY! THERE'S MINE! THERE'S
MINE!" I hollered very excited. "MINE IS

THE GRAMPA WITH THE BALDIE
HEAD!"

"Mine too!" said a girl named Charlotte.

"Mine too!" said my boyfriend named
Ricardo.

Then a grandma with blond hair came in.
And she had on long red fingernails. And
dangling earrings with jewels on them.

"That's my nanna!" said Lucille.

I smiled at her. "Your nanna looks like a
moneybags, Lucille," I said.

After that, another grandma came in.
And she runned over to that Jim I hate. And
she tried to hug him very tight.

Only that mean Jim just kept on standing
there. And he didn't even hug her back.

I tapped on her.

"I will hug you," I said.

And so then me and her hugged real tight.

61

"I hate your grandboy," I said very sweet.

Just then Mrs. clapped her loud hands together. And she made the grandparents sit down in the back of the room.

Then the children talked all about what we do in Room Nine.

"It is fun here," said my bestest friend, that Grace. "We learn to count. And to read. And to wash our hands after we go to the bathroom."

"And we learn recess and snacks and art," said Ricardo.

"Art is my favorite," I called out. "Only my art didn't get hanged up. 'Cause I painted a horse. And his head turned out like a fat wiener sausage. And so I had to tear it up and stomp on it with my shoes."

Then that mean Jim did a cuckoo sign at me.

And it was right in front of the whole entire grandparents!

"Yeah, only everybody makes mistakes!" I said. "Right, Mrs.? Right? 'Cause on Saturday you kissed a strange man at the grocery store. And then you stoled a bunch of grapes. And so even teachers make mistakes. Right?"

Mrs.'s face went funny. Then her skin turned the color of reddish. And her voice couldn't say any words.

"How come you're not talking, Mrs.?" I hollered out. "Does the dead cat got your tongue?"

Just then Grandma Miller made a loud laugh in the back of the room.

Then I heard my grampa laugh, too.

And pretty soon, lots of other grandparents were laughing and laughing.

"HEY! IT SOUNDS HAPPY IN THIS PLACE!" I hollered.

After that, Mrs. didn't look so reddish anymore.

Then we got out the 'freshments. And Grandma Miller helped me put my cookies on a plate.

Mrs. made a 'nouncement to Room Nine. And she said only two cookies apiece for the children.

Except for I ate four delicious chocolate ones. And nobody even saw me!

Only that's not called stealing.

That's called *extras*.

After the 'freshments, the grandparents had to go home to their houses.

And so I hugged my grandma and grandpa very much.

And then I hugged that mean Jim's grandma too.

And also Lucille's moneybags nanna.

"Love your earrings," I said.

Then Mrs. saw me being polite. And she smiled very nice at me.

Mrs. has white teeth.

They are just like Grampa Miller's teeth. Only hers don't come out, I think.

Except I'm not for sure positive.

And so guess what?

I still wish I could hide in her hamper.

That's what.

Books are my very **FAVORITE** things in the whole world! I have *lots* of funny stories to share! Laugh out loud with books like these. . . .

BARBARA PARK
Junie B. Jones
and the
Yucky Blucky Fruitcake

BARBARA PARK
Junie B. Jones
and That
Meanie Jim's
Birthday

Junie B. Jones

Junie B.'s Sticker Scrapbook Sensation to Spark Your 'Magination!
(Psst! And It's FREE!)

Do You Want . . .

- a special book to save your favorite Junie B. stickers from the new foil-covered paperbacks?
- a perfect place to paste and draw your memories from this year?
- lots of happy, creative scrapbook tips from Junie B.?

YES! YES! YES!

(You can get it FREE at participating retailers and online at www.randomhouse.com/junieb)

Here are some of Junie B.'s favorite photos from her *own* sticker scrapbook!

Bestest Good Friends!

Uh-oh! I'm in Trouble!

RANDOM HOUSE
CHILDREN'S BOOKS

Wowie wow wow!
I'm so glad you're my pal!
Let's play at my Web site.
I'll meet you there now!

www.randomhouse.com/kids/junieb

Don't miss these other great books by Barbara Park!

Rah! Rah! Rah!
Join the crowd.
Read these books
And laugh out loud!

Junie B. has a lot to say . . .

the baby's room
Mother and Daddy fixed up a room for the new baby.
It's called a nursery. Except I don't know why. Because
a baby isn't a nurse, of course.
• from *Junie B. Jones and a Little Monkey Business*

school words
After that, the mop got removed from us. *Removed* is
the school word for snatched right out of our hands.
• from *Junie B. Jones and Her Big Fat Mouth*

rules
Me and Mother had a little talk. It was called—*no
screaming back off, clown.* Only I never even heard of
that rule before.
• from *Junie B. Jones and the Yucky Blucky Fruitcake*

her baby brother
His name is Ollie. I love him a real lot. Except I wish he
didn't live at my actual house.
• from *Junie B. Jones and That Meanie Jim's Birthday*

saving a seat
Saving a seat is when you zoom on the bus. And you hurry up and sit down. And then you quick put your feet on the seat next to you. After that, you keep on screaming the word "SAVED! SAVED! SAVED!" And no one even sits next to you. 'Cause who wants to sit next to a screamer? That's what I would like to know.
• from *Junie B. Jones Loves Handsome Warren*

twirling
I twirled and twirled all over the kitchen. Only too bad for me. 'Cause I accidentally twirled into the refrigerator and the stove and the dishwasher.
• from *Junie B. Jones Is a Beauty Shop Guy*

cribs
A crib is a bed with bars on the side of it. It's kind of like a cage at the zoo. Except with a crib, you can put your hand through the bars. And the baby won't pull you in and kill you.
• from *Junie B. Jones and a Little Monkey Business*

. . . in Barbara Park's
Junie B. Jones books!

ideas

Just then, I smiled real big. 'Cause a great idea popped in my head, that's why! It came right out of thin hair!

• from *Junie B. Jones Is a Party Animal*

punishment

Grounded, young lady is when I have to stay on my own ground. Plus also, I can go on the rug.

• from *Junie B. Jones Is Not a Crook*

apologies

A 'pology is the words *I'm sorry.* Except for you don't actually have to mean it. 'Cause nobody can even tell the difference.

• from *Junie B. Jones and Some Sneaky Peeky Spying*

school

Kindergarten is where you go to meet new friends and not watch TV.

• from *Junie B. Jones and the Stupid Smelly Bus*